MIKE YOUNG

SUPERTED

AT THE BOTTOM OF THE SEA

Illustrations by
Bryan Jones, Chris Kinsey and Andrew Offiler

Muller

In his space station SuperTed has a powerful video-scanner which can pick up messages from all over the world.

'Help! Help!' A boy was trying to contact SuperTed from the middle of the ocean.

SuperTed quickly said the secret, magic word and at once changed into the brave superbear. In a flash, he flew out of the space station and down towards the sea.

SuperTed to the rescue!

The signal was coming from a little boat, full of diving equipment. In the boat was a boy called Andrew, who looked very upset.

'My two friends went diving for treasure and haven't come back,' said Andrew.

'Don't worry,' said SuperTed, with a kind smile. 'Put on your diving equipment and come with me. We'll find them and bring them back safely.'

He took Andrew's hand, and they dived into the cool, clear water.

The current was very strong. It swept SuperTed and Andrew towards a beautiful coral reef. Andrew's breathing equipment became entangled in a piece of long coral. He struggled and struggled but could not get free.

SuperTed calmed Andrew and quickly swam away. Then a few seconds later he returned, riding on the back of a swordfish. The helpful fish cut through the coral to allow Andrew to escape.

Soon the current slowed. There, on the bottom of the sea, lay a Spanish galleon. It was covered with sand and seaweed, and long, slimy eels with sharp teeth slithered in and out of the tattered rigging.

Andrew was frightened, but he stayed close to SuperTed and swam nearer to the galleon. He knew they had to find his missing friends.

SuperTed examined the ship carefully. Suddenly he caught sight of a stream of bubbles rising from the other side of the ship.

SuperTed could see the two frightened faces looking through a narrow crack in the deck of the ship. They had found the boys. When they saw SuperTed and Andrew, the two boys waved frantically and tried to shout.

'Bu-bubble! Bu-bubble!' Their shouts spluttered in the water.

SuperTed could see that they were trapped. With a piece of broken mast he managed to lever up a plank in the deck of the ship.

The inside of the ship was full of precious jewels. SuperTed recognised them. They had been stolen from a London museum. But he had no time to look at them now. His first task was to get the boys back safely to their boat.

Just as they were swimming out of the ship a large eel slithered out of the darkness and coiled itself around SuperTed. He spun round at tremendous speed to unwind the eel, and then shook it like a whip. When he let go, the eel wobbled away, looking very frightened.

Once they had reached the boat, SuperTed asked the boys how they had been trapped.

'We dived into the ship and found the jewels,' said the boys, 'but then someone bolted down all the hatches and locked us in.'

Before the boys could say any more, a large black object suddenly rose out of the water and overturned their boat. It was a submarine.

A man dressed as a cowboy stood on the deck of the submarine and laughed at them. It was Texas Pete.

'Ha! Ha! Ha! So you got away, did you? Well, you may have found my hide-out but you will never be clever enough to catch me,' he said. Then he climbed back into his submarine and sped away.

SuperTed first turned the boat the right way up and helped the boys to climb back in. Then he flew off in pursuit of the submarine.

SuperTed could see the submarine's periscope sticking up out of the water. He flew down and covered it with his paws.

Texas Pete could not see where he was going, and crashed the submarine into a large rock. He rose to the surface inside a huge bubble.

His cowboy clothes were very wet.

When he saw SuperTed, he started kicking and splashing.

'You haven't caught me yet, SuperTed,' he yelled. 'I'm not afraid of a teddy bear.'

SuperTed grabbed him by the arms and pushed him through the water at great speed until he found a friendly octopus. He wrapped Texas Pete in its tentacles, and told the octopus to hold on to him until the police came.

The police were very pleased that SuperTed had caught Texas Pete. They had been looking for him for a long time, but had never suspected that he might be hiding under the sea.

They asked SuperTed and the boys to help their police divers fetch all the stolen jewels up from the Spanish galleon.

Later, SuperTed and the boys took the jewels back to the museum.

'Thank you very much, SuperTed,' said the museum curator. 'These jewels are very beautiful. They belong here where everyone can come and see them.'

Long queues of people visit the museum every day to look at the jewels. And now on the side of the display case is a little brass plaque which says: Thank you, SuperTed.

Books in the SuperTed series